New Year's

Miracle

Book 4 of the Stonewater Stories

By

Ginny Frost

Copyright

This is a work of fiction. Names, characters, places, and incidents are either the product of the author's imagination or are used fictitiously, and any resemblance to actual persons living or dead, business establishments, events, or locales, is entirely coincidental.

New Year's Miracle

Contact Information: **ginnyfrost@ginnyfrost.com**
Ginny Frost
PO Box 4686
Halfmoon, NY 12065-9211

Visit me at **ginnyfrost.com**
Published in the United States of America
Edited by **Sandra Nguyen of Untangled Yarns: Fiction and Nonfiction**
Cover Image via depositphotos.com by aletia

Acknowledgements

I'd like to thank my editor, Sandra for getting all these books out so quickly. She's a miracle. Also, I'd like to thank my coworkers. Thank you for your support and kindness.

Dedication

This book is for everyone who discovered talking about the problem usually solves it.
Love to you all.

Chapter One

"What are you doing here?" Beverly Winston-Bristol clutched at the top of her sweater set. The open door revealed the last person she wanted to see tonight, David Kramer. The idea of the man at her home sent a war of emotions through her. Aggravation won.

How dare he?

David stood on her doorstep, dressed in an old parka, his toolbox at his side. His rugged face sported a wide grin, and his brown eyes twinkled in the glow from her porch light.

"You gonna let me in?" he asked.

"Certainly not."

Even with Father gone, Bev hesitated to invite David into her home. He'd never been inside before. Thirty-five plus years of animosity between them said he should remain outside. And with the problems she'd already encountered tonight? *No, thank you.*

Fifteen minutes ago, the five-thousand-dollar limited-edition crib for Bev's new granddaughter collapsed with a resounding bang. Five-month-old Harper, who'd been blissfully sleeping in her arms, woke with a shriek that rattled the rafters. With a screaming baby (*one she just found out about, thank you very much*) and nowhere for the child to sleep, Bev called her daughter, Cheryl, immediately.

Now, the bane of her existence stood on her doorstep instead.

David watched her with his same steady gaze. He never questioned people, nagged, or dug for answers. He looked at people, and they confessed their souls.

Bev gripped her collar tighter. She'd last seen him at dinner on Christmas Eve with the Porter family. Nice enough, but very middle class. The woman, Daisy, cooked the entire meal herself, a ridiculous amount of work for one person. If anyone had bothered to tell Bev ahead of time, she would've hired a caterer immediately.

With a caterer on duty, Bev would've avoided the ordeal of washing dishes with the talkative little boy before David rescued her.

David rescued…

No. She wouldn't think about it. She would not consider how he carefully took the dishtowel from her or how he'd said, "Looks like the rest needs some elbow grease. Let me." She ignored the flutter in her chest as his breath warmed her skin. Probably, the over-sauced asparagus caused her heartburn.

Now, on her doorstep, David held a toolbox. "You called Cheryl about the baby bed?"

Bev looked at him dumbly. After the crib fell apart, she phoned her daughter on speed dial. She didn't care if it was New Year's Eve, and Cheryl was out on a date with Ted, David's son. Bev had nothing for the child to sleep in. She informed Cheryl she must come and take the baby.

Why was David here?

"I called her, but…"

David shrugged. "Ted called me." He rattled the toolbox. "At your service, Mrs. Winston-Bristol." He produced a heart-warming grin.

Bev worked hard not to see the young man whose smile once melted her heart.

She stared at him for a minute before holding up her hand. "Where's the travel bed? If Cheryl's not coming for Harper, I require a portable crib."

David shrugged. "Don't know. They said the crib needed fixing, and here I am." Again with the smile.

Her hand fluttered to her collar. "No, no. It won't work. You can't come in and repair the crib. Where will I put the baby?"

"Where do you got her now?" He tilted his head to peek past her.

In the parlor, Harper sat in her bouncy chair, buckled tight. Bev had racked her brain to think of what else to do with her.

"Cheryl usually has... It's my first..." She cut herself off, not wanting David Kramer, of all people, to assume she'd never watched her granddaughter before— or that she didn't know how to take care of her.

If only Cheryl had allowed her to hire a nanny... But now Bev had a pile of rubble for her little grandchild to sleep in, and no one but a Kramer to help her.

She checked the thought.

In the two weeks since she'd learned about Harper, her life had become a rollercoaster. Not to mention the shock of learning the child's parentage, but Bev had gotten her own daughter back after a year's absence. Those two weeks had changed Bev so much.

Of course, the dozens of conversations with Cheryl set the tone. She handed down an ultimatum—if Bev didn't find a way to get along with the Kramers, she'd be banned from seeing Harper.

Bev was trying. She did the Christmas Eve thing and invited Ted for her own Christmas dinner. Adding one more plate hadn't been too much of a problem. The conversation, on the other hand, felt stilted and difficult. Mostly, she, Cheryl, Ted, Will, and Mother cooed at the baby and talked about childcare.

Well, except for Will. As usual, he kept himself to himself, but lately, he appeared a little withdrawn. *It's his first Christmas without Father. He probably misses him.*

"You want me to fix the crib?"

David's words broke into her thoughts, and Bev moved aside to allow him into her home for the first time. He stopped in the foyer and gazed around, a slight smile on his lips. "Fancy," he said. "Where's Harper?"

Her mouth hung open, and anger bubbled in her blood. *How dare he dismiss her elegant home?*

The open foyer had marble flooring, mahogany trim, the perfect sand-colored wallpaper, and an antique credenza all the neighbors envied. She'd spent years—without help from Mother or Cheryl—decorating the house to perfection, to create the right impression for Father's friends and guests.

And David called it "fancy."

No wonder they never worked out.

She shook her head to check her feelings. He was like any other service worker to help with a project. Never mind any past emotional ties or how cute he looked in his parka.

That reminded her, "Let me take your coat," she offered, hoping to sound like a congenial hostess.

"Oh, sure," he said, putting the toolbox down and sliding off his parka. Their hands briefly touched as she took the garment. Warmth poured over her skin where their fingers touched. Quickly, she hung it in the closet, willing her heartbeat to slow. *How could this old man have such an effect on me after thirty-five years?*

"Harper's in here," she said, pointing to the parlor.

Harper sat in a chair that was purported to be supportive, educational, and bouncy. Her rosy complexion glowed as her brown eyes scanned the room, taking in everything. The child had managed to trap one arm under the strap and pull off both her socks.

How in the world?

David laughed at the sight. "The kid hates socks."

How did he know that already? Bev glanced at him, then back to Harper. "I guess I should've used the baby bag or the pajamas with the feet. But seriously, they look so... undignified."

"Baby bag?" he asked, his head cocked like a spaniel.

She waved her hands. "It's like a nightgown, but the bottom is sewed closed. Cheryl said Harper was too old for it. But she's so tiny."

"She is small," David agreed. "Were your kids that tiny?"

"Oh, yes. Both weighed five pounds at birth." She opened her mouth to continue, but recalled to whom she was speaking and closed her lips. Not the time to walk down memory lane, especially with him. Not to mention, the less she shared about her inability to care for Harper, the better.

A pause hung in the air as they both gazed at Harper, who sang at the toys hanging over her head. She must not have realized her arm was trapped.

A sharp babble from Harper snapped Bev out of her reverie. She rushed forward to release the arm in case the baby began howling again. That child could make noise to wake the dead. That's why she'd called Cheryl. The baby was inconsolable after the crash of the crib. Now she seemed fine. Perhaps Bev had acted too soon.

"Where's the crib?" David asked.

The remains of it sat upstairs in the new nursery she'd hastily put together with the help of the Neiman Marcus consultant. She hadn't had time to design the room, much less obtain custom furniture. The store contained an excellent selection, but the Cinderella carriage crib was the only choice for Harper. The price seemed a tad bit high, considering what they received. Ted said he'd build something for Bev, but never followed through. He'd waited a week already to finish building something.

She stepped toward the stairs with David behind her, but the idea of him near her bedroom stopped her cold. "I suppose I can put her down to sleep in the chair or her car seat."

He glanced at her sideways, studying her. "I'm here. Might as well let me look at the bed."

She tightened her arms around her chest.

David being upstairs was… unprecedented.

He sighed. "I promise not to poke into your things if I go up there."

Always with the jokes, these Kramers.

Resigned, Bev dropped her chin to her chest and pointed up the mahogany stairway.

David took his time climbing the enormous staircase. He'd been in the Winston mansion a few times, but only at the servants' entrance. With her pa gone, and only she and Evangeline in the house, would that door still be in use? Cheryl still lived in an apartment in New Delphi, and Will stayed at his school. Bev's empty nest was the size of an airplane hangar.

And, of course, he failed to stop his critical eye from finding a few things in need of repair—a loose finial, a crack on the ceiling. He stopped. Even now, being kin, Beverly would never hire him to fix things.

'Course, he could offer…

He waited at the top of the stairs for her, watching her wring her hands and look anywhere but at him. His ego reveled in the fact that she refused to look him square in the eye. She'd done so a couple times at Daisy's dinner, but only for a second. Hell, he'd led her into the dining room that night. The memory brought a smile to his lips.

He glanced at Bev. Tonight, her outfit and hair screamed sophistication and style. Her light-blue sweater was almost the same color as her beautiful eyes. He was careful not to admire her trim figure or delicate hands. Bev was still stunning in her late fifties.

"What are you grinning at?" she snapped, making total eye contact.

He turned his gaze to her pretty face. "Just waiting on instructions. I didn't wanna get lost."

She strolled past him, brushing off his comment. "Please, it's not that big, David."

The double meaning of her comment hit his funny bone, and he pressed his lips tight to repress a snicker.

One did not make dirty jokes in front of the likes of Beverly Winston-Bristol.

As she reached a door midway down the hall, her hand on the doorknob, Harper shrieked with laughter.

"Oh, my God. I left the baby alone." She clutched at her throat again.

David shook his head. "She sounds happy and is locked down in that contraption. She's fine."

Bev glanced from the stairs to him and back to the stairs, worry coloring her expression. "Do you think?"

"Long enough for you to show me to the room and get back to her." He hoped his cool tone eased her fear. Hadn't she raised two little ones? Nah, she probably hired a slew of nannies and maids. He swallowed. Ugly thoughts wouldn't ease the tension between them.

Think about Harper.

"In here," she said. She opened the door and dashed down the stairs in record time.

David shook his head. *First grandkid. Bev will get the hang of it soon.*

He marched down the hall to the open door and stood for a moment, taking in the decor. A flowery wallpaper covered the walls on three sides, with the fourth wall painted bubble-gum pink. Frilly lace curtains covered the windows, and David had never seen so many stuffed animals. Everything looked store-bought, catalog-perfect, and brand-spanking-new.

Except for the large pile of metal rods in the center of the room. He guessed by the mattress in the middle, it used to be the crib. He squinted his eyes and turned his head back and forth. The pile gave no indication of the rectangular shape he'd expected.

He put his toolbox on the floor and squatted in front of the metallic heap, inspecting the pieces closest to him. Three large hoops and four wagon wheels lay among what looked like cage pieces.

What the…?

As he pulled a wheel from the pile, Bev's voice sounded behind him.

"Can you fix it?" she asked, worry colored her words.

Her wide eyes held a hint of trepidation, but she carried Harper with confidence. The child looked thrilled to be in her grammy's arms, squeaking and babbling, reaching for her hair and face. Harper was the happiest kid he'd ever seen.

He smiled at her.

Bev blinked at him, looked behind her, and then locked gazes. "What?"

He turned his gaze to the metal rods. "Nothing. The kid's cute." He focused on pulling the various pieces from the pile and stacking them neatly. He refrained from thinking about Bev Winston-Bristol holding their grandbaby, and what a beautiful picture it made.

"You got a diagram of what this used to look like? Because I don't have a clue." He stood and waved a hand over the pile of metal. *Ted needs to build a real crib, and soon.*

Bev walked over and stood next to him. She wrinkled her nose. "Try the internet? I don't have any of the boxes or instructions."

David pulled out the fancy phone Brett bought him. Jo, Brett's new girl, had shown David how to use it. Most of the lessons went over his head. He could play solitaire, get email, and do simple searches. He hit the circle rainbow button for the internet.

"Where did you get the bed?" he asked. A picture might give him an idea of how to fix it. If he wanted instructions, he'd call Ted to snatch 'em off a website.

"*A-BéBé* in Brooklyn," she said, giving Harper a little jiggle. The kid's eyelids began to droop as she played with Grandma's hair. Bev never fussed at her to stop. "It's the Cinderella's carriage."

"Seriously?" He laughed. "Wasn't it supposed to wait until midnight to collapse?"

Bev's dead expression and tight lips said she didn't appreciate his joke.

He sighed, glancing at the pile of metal. *Why buy something this fancy for a baby? And from Brooklyn?* Target sold tons of simple, practical cribs. Giant wagon wheels on a baby bed didn't sound safe.

"*A-BéBé*." She spelled it for him, leaning over his shoulder to view the phone screen. He typed it in, glad of something to focus on other than Bev's perfume. The scent fed his soul, and he drank it in.

He hadn't been this close to her in over thirty-five years. Apparently, she wore the same scent. Chanel No.5 always brought him back to warm summer nights in the back of his convertible, holding her hand and gazing at the stars. How could the woman rev his engine after all these years? Perhaps the baby in her arms had something to do with it.

"That's it," she said, breaking his daydream.

David stared at the image of a metal cage with the hoops creating the shape of a pumpkin and with wheels on the sides. The thing looked like a little girl's perfect fantasy. Cute, but over the top. Then he caught the price.

"Huh," he stammered, unsure what to say. He glanced at the metal, processing that number. For that price, the contraption should've lasted a hundred years. Oh, well. It was Bev's choice to spend her money however she wished.

"I bet one of these wheels fell off or something." He studied the picture and the parts, putting it together in his head. He must have taken too long, because Bev groaned in frustration.

"Go over to Macy's in Iverton and buy me a new one. I'll give you money for it."

David chuckled again. Bev couldn't be so clueless, but then, she never really grasped the real world. "It's eight o'clock on New Year's Eve. Nothing's open."

"Well, call, and see…"

"Bev," he said in the authoritative voice he used on the boys when they messed up. Not loud, but strong. "Nobody's open now. It's New Year's Eve. Either the baby sleeps in the car seat…"

Bev wrinkled her nose as if it constituted an unjust punishment for the kiddo.

"…or I put this thing back together." He waved a hand at the mess. "I wish you'da bought a wooden crib, though."

"Can you fix it?" She glanced from the baby to the metal to him in a round-robin. Her eyebrows knitted with worry, and her lips disappeared into a thin line.

"Sure." He shrugged, a little surprised she wanted him to stay. She still hated him. For what reason, he had no idea. She'd walked out on him.

Chapter Two

"I'll give ya a holler when it's done," David said.

Bev sighed. "Fine. I'll change her while we're here."

He examined both the metal pile and the photo of the carriage on his phone while tossing glances at Bev from the corner of his eye. His attempts to help with the baby failed as Bev commented diapers were "women's work." He scoffed hard, but she refused to allow him to help.

He and his late wife Joan shared the chores from kids to laundry to the yard. Nothing at their house was "women's work." They both did it all. After she passed, it was all him. 'Course by then, the boys were practically adults, mid-teens, and Ted had filled in like a trooper.

Once Bev changed her, Harper resumed her usual squirming, giggling ways. Bev headed for the door. "I'll take her downstairs. She'll never sleep with you banging away on the bed."

David pressed his lips, hiding the wide grin that wanted to spread across his face. Her second double entendre of the night almost threw him into laughing fits.

When he said nothing, her double meaning must have dawned on her. Bev's face turned beet red, and she fussed, "You know what I mean. I'm taking her downstairs to tire her out."

He tapped one of the cage pieces with his foot. "Wish I had instructions…"

She looked over her shoulder at the door. "You have a fancy phone. Have it find them."

David doubted he could find the directions, much less read them on the phone without his glasses. Calling Brett or Ted seemed out, as it was date night for both of them. But he'd give it a go. If it didn't work, he'd take Harper to his place and put her in a dresser drawer as they did for Ryan when he was small.

He pulled the cloth sheets and mattress from the pile and tossed them in the corner. He examined the rest. If he removed the wheels and the hoops, it resembled an oblong metal rectangle. He could fix it. He bent over and got to work.

Five minutes later, the sound of a fussy baby trailed up the stairs. David listened as he attempted to screw one metal grid into another. Of course, the stress of the collapse had bent the screws every which way. He rummaged through his toolbox for better hardware rather than the shitty pieces that came with the bed.

No wonder it collapsed.

He took a minute to sit on his heels and suss out the entire situation. He was helping Bev in her own home. Maybe miracles could happen.

With her father passed, the house seemed lighter. Not that he'd ever been this deep inside, but the atmosphere around the place felt comfortable. The house was a handyman's dream. Minor projects lingered everywhere. Despite only viewing three rooms, he saw little problems everywhere. He could spend his entire retirement helping Bev out.

Anyway… Maybe now they would bury the hatchet and move on. Thirty-five years was long enough to fight over a bad break-up. Her dad no longer had the power to dismiss David's worth or tell his daughter the Kramers were beneath her. And Evangeline liked him. With

Harper as an insulator, there might be more nights like tonight, more dinners like at Daisy's, more time to talk.

A loud howl sounded from downstairs, an epithet from Bev, and then serious baby crying. With a sigh, he put down his screwdriver and headed downstairs.

Bev scooped little Harper off the floor. The play mat with the adorable animal pictures just did not suit her tonight. She glanced at the clock with a sigh. The baby was overdue for bedtime, and Cheryl wouldn't be home for hours.

Bev pressed the crying baby to her chest, and the heat of the little one's anger steamed out. Usually, Harper was such a quiet child. She slept most of the time, and when awake, she was happy and quite cute.

Not tonight, of course—tonight when Bev tried her hardest to be a good grandmother, tonight when David Kramer was in her house. He'd take one look at how Bev failed with Harper and thank his lucky stars they'd never married. She'd have been a terrible mother without Father's money to hire nannies and babysitters.

Bev rocked the little one back and forth, trying to soothe, but tears formed in her own eyes. "We can do this, my sweetie. We can. Tell Grandma what you need."

At the word "grandma," Harper lifted her head and looked Bev straight in the eye. She reached out a hand and touched Bev's lips. Automatically, Bev kissed the tiny hand. A smile lit Harper's brown eyes for a second.

They stood there, eye to eye, hand to mouth. Something clicked in Bev's chest. This little girl represented their future. She held the path to peace in the family. One little baby had put her and David at the same dinner table, and in the same house on New Year's Eve. Perhaps next year would bring a fresh start for everyone.

The moment lasted but a second as Harper's mouth curled into a frown, and she sniffled. Bev pressed the child to her shoulder and did the jiggly walk Cheryl taught her.

It didn't work.

David padded down the stairs, as quietly as possible.

Bev paced back and forth across the room filled with stuffy furniture. Harper's bright red face hovered over Bev's shoulder. After a long shriek, the baby opened her eyes and caught sight of David peeking from the foyer. The baby gulped, hiccupped, and made frantic motions with her arms as if reaching out for him.

David walked into the room and held his arms out for the kiddo.

Bev pressed her lips and rolled her eyes, but handed over the cranky baby.

"I think someone's hungry," he said, and Bev huffed.

"Fine. She took a bottle two hours ago. But what do I know about babies?"

"About as much as me," David said, giving her a little hip-check. "We'll muddle through."

Bev ushered him into the kitchen.

He stopped in the doorway and goggled at the size. *You could cook a meal for an army in here.* Not that Bev cooked—she preferred to be waited on. There was something old-fashioned and endearing about it, if you overlooked the spoiled-brat factor.

She motioned to another store-bought contraption that resembled a highchair. He placed Harper in the seat and buckled her in. The chair appeared complicated, and ridiculously huge for tiny Harper. He'd have to poke Ted about making a good seat for his girl's visits to Grandma.

Bev moved through the motions of making a bottle while David made faces at Harper.

The baby smiled and kicked until the last silly expression caused her to squeal with joy. The sharp sound threw Bev off. She barely caught the bottle before she dropped it.

"Oh, God. She scared the life out of me. Stop making her scream," Bev grimaced but gathered herself. She'd always been quick with a barb. He admired her spunk, though it annoyed most everyone else. "And what are you still doing in here? The bed is not going to repair itself."

David glanced at her, then at the baby. "You want Grandpa to leave?"

Harper whooped and whistled. The two had bonded instantly, which made no sense. The kiddo should be all over her grandma and great gran, since they smelled more like Cheryl. No matter.

"Why are you asking an infant?" Bev walked over and handed the bottle to Harper. It promptly fell to the floor. Bev blinked, and David tried not to laugh as he retrieved it.

"You've never fed her?"

Bev crossed her arms. "Last time I fed her, I held her. She's five months. Why isn't she holding her own bottle by now?"

David shrugged. "Harper's her own girl."

The baby looked at his face, then the bottle and back. She held her hands out and made the sweetest little begging noise.

David laughed as he crossed to the sink, where he ran the nipple under hot water.

"You can't do that. It hit the floor. We have to make a fresh bottle."

Harper began to fuss.

"Nah, hot kills the germs. Nothing got inside. We'd spend all day cleaning if we scrubbed everything she threw to the floor."

"She throws things but can't hold the bottle?"

"She's a baby." David shook his head. He released Harper from the seat contraption and carried her out of the kitchen into the sitting room.

Bev scowled at David's back. Why wasn't he fixing the crib? She was alone in the mansion with him and the baby—no one to call for help. Not that David acted threatening or dangerous. He was annoyingly not doing the job she asked him to do.

In the parlor, he settled into one of the wingback chairs, Harper on his lap. He whispered to her quietly, the bottle poised over her mouth. The little beauty squealed and reached. David relented and gave her the nipple.

Bev stood in the doorway, her emotions mixed. While she appreciated a babysitting helper, she didn't want a Kramer here, especially David. Christmas dinner was fine enough with a whole brood of people eating and talking. But the two of them alone in her house? She crossed her arms and shivered at the idea.

She had nothing to say to this man, not after he'd hurt her so badly. Even if they were grandparents together.

David's gaze fixed on the small bundle in his arms. Harper stared back at him. Cheryl mentioned he'd been successful in calming the little girl.

Without glancing up, he said, "Can you find me a towel? She'll need a burp soon enough."

"Must you be so crude? You were always crude." She fussed and searched the giant satchel Cheryl brought. Everything was strewn about, mixed together. *Why wasn't Cheryl more organized?* Then Bev remembered she herself had trashed the bag, searching for the sucky thing. A binkie, Cheryl called it. God, babies were a lesson in patience, organization, and vocabulary.

David glanced over at her, and she tucked her head, not wanting him to witness her struggle.

She regretted giving the maid the evening off. New Year's Eve constituted a minor holiday, but she hated playing the scrooge. *I can do it, even with David here.*

"Babies burp, Bev. And Harper… She eats too fast. Half of what she swallows is air."

Bev harrumphed and brought out a small piece of cloth. It looked like an old-fashioned diaper, but lavender with little stitched flowers. "Is this what you require?"

She moved to toss it at him. One glance at Harper's little pink face calmed her anger.

She crossed the room and held the towel out like a peace offering.

As he took it from her hand, his fingers grazed hers.

Heat shot up her neck to her cheeks. It wasn't fair David Kramer's touch still heated her skin after thirty-five years.

"Thanks," he said, his low voice sending shivers down her spine. "Did you forget this stuff from when yours were little?" He adjusted Harper to his shoulder on top of the carefully placed towel and stood.

Bev hopped back a step, surprised by his quick movements.

He grinned. "Didn't want to get anything on such a fine chair," he said and moved around the room, patting Harper's back.

"Thank you," she said. The embarrassment and uncomfortableness of the situation pulled her off balance. She sat on the wingback's ottoman and folded her hands in her lap. *Might as well embrace it*. He appeared to be a whiz with babies, and she needed the help.

After a few minutes and an enormous belch from the baby, David settled back in the chair, bottle in hand.

Again, Harper extended her arms toward it.

"Are you forcing her to reach?"

"Yep. She's tiny, but won't be for long." He smiled warmly at her.

Bev's stomach clenched and she looked away, her emotions tumbling over each other. She loved seeing Harper happy, but David had brought out the happy. She and David might be spending much more time together than the occasional meal.

Being grandparents together might be a problem.

They sat quietly, not speaking while the baby worked through the second half of her meal.

A bottle meant another change, which would wake Harper up. Bev glanced around, realizing they'd have to carry the baby upstairs again. *What a pain.* First thing on Monday, she'd call the decorator to redesign the nursery. She now realized the room lacked stations for feeding, changing, and rocking. Plus, the ridiculous crib must go. She sighed.

"The crib's finished?" she asked, not looking up.

"No, I heard her fussing and realized it was a 'food' cry. Thought I'd help." He glanced up. "Want her back? I'll go finish upstairs."

Bev bit her lip. Harper remained quiet and sweet with David. *Best not to upset the apple cart.* "No, finish the bottle. Then we'll do the crib afterward."

The two sat quietly as the baby gulped her late-night snack. Bev watched, a little jealous of their bond. She sighed heavily.

David glanced at her for a second. "That sounded ominous. Penny for your thoughts." He met her gaze, and heat rushed over her again.

"All the baby business… the equipment… Cheryl hasn't committed to moving home. I don't know what I need or how much. And the room upstairs… the crib is all wrong." She threw her hands up in the air, stood, and paced.

David said nothing.

"It's been such an upheaval. My father's death, the baby…" She glanced at David, and trying not to offend, said in a weak voice, "her parentage…"

"Yeah, it's been a rough couple of weeks, Bev. Sorry it got thrown at you all at once."

As Harper emptied the last of the formula, her eyes rolled up, and she fell asleep.

David chuckled low. "She seems to do that when she's stuffed. Wonder if it will stay with her."

Bev smiled at the sleeping child, her heart filling with warmth. It wasn't the way she'd planned to become a grandmother. Not the way she wanted her life to turn out. Not the man she wanted her daughter to settle with.

But Harper was precious. Bev reached out and rubbed her fingers along Harper's cheek. The baby made a sucking motion in her sleep and cuddled into David with a soft sigh.

What a beautiful sight.

David caught her eye. "You've been through a lot, but I could use some help upstairs. Then we can talk about the elephant in the room."

Chapter Three

David knew he was shit-stirring. But after years of waiting for her to say something, anything, he saw a chance and took it. They'd avoided being alone for longer than a flash in thirty-plus years. Even after all this time, he wanted to understand her choice.

"Elephant?" she asked, pretending not to understand what he meant. She feigned that she didn't have a clue, when she knew exactly what she was doing. She caught his gaze, and he flashed her a full, robust grin. And she laughed—actually laughed.

"Which one?" she asked with a smirk. "Our kids dating? Our new granddaughter? My father's death?"

He twitched his mouth, wishing he'd brought a toothpick. Ever since he quit smoking fifteen years ago, he always carried a toothpick. When anxiety hit, he popped it in his mouth. It worked better than a cigarette to soothe his nerves.

"Lady's choice?"

Was he asking her? Be nice to end the damned feud for good. Especially with little Harper at stake.

He glanced down at her, then to Bev, who also stared at the sleeping baby.

"You're marvelous with her." A ghost of a smile crossed Bev's lips.

"Calm begets calm."

She dodged that question. He wasn't surprised. Bev had been dodging him since he'd asked her to marry him.

The two sat in silence for a while, with Harper sleeping on David's chest. *Life should always be this good*. He glanced at the car seat. It'd only take a second to place Harper in it and bring her home. Problem solved for both of them.

Before he moved, Bev spoke, "Will it work?"

"Getting her to sleep tonight? Ain't we already done it?" He smiled and shifted. Harper's eyes blinked open for a millisecond and closed again. "Let's give her a good ten minutes before putting her in the car seat or bouncy chair." *That should be enough time to clear the air, right?*

"I mean Ted and Cheryl. I'm not sure how it will go. She's so… headstrong, and he's…" She waved a hand.

"He's in love."

Bev looked away, her cheeks pink.

"Ted ain't never fallen before. When she left town, you'da thought someone shot his puppy." He chuckled. "Never seen him so happy as when he introduced us to Harper."

Bev stared at her hands, not meeting his gaze. "Did you know about them dating?"

David shook his head. "No, but I did think it took a long time to finish the porch on the carriage house."

She rolled her eyes. "My mother hired him…" She waved a hand, as if placing the blame on Evangeline.

He chuckled. "I remember your ma did the same thing thirty-ought years ago. What did she hire me for?" He tapped his chin as if he didn't remember the job exactly. Would Beverly recall?

"That stupid gazebo in the garden." She huffed, arms crossed in her lap. She gifted him one glance before she looked away again. "If I remember correctly, it took you a while to finish." This time, she stared at him pointedly before sliding her gaze to the sleeping baby.

"Yeah, well, a cute girl brought me lemonade. Plus, I had to ask my pa about some stuff."

Bev's brow furrowed. "Why didn't your father complete the job and save my family the money?" *Did regret color her words?* Her question lacked any real strength. Instead, it sounded desperate and forlorn.

"Because I told him about the girl and the lemonade." He grinned.

Bev blushed.

"David…"

And as always, Bev Winston-Bristol saying his name sent a thrill over his skin. A sensation he hadn't felt since high school, and it still brought a blush to his cheeks.

"I hoped your ma would hire us for more projects, but your dad chased me off once he got wind of…" He held out a hand toward her and lowered his head.

Bev sighed. She glanced out the window into the garden. Moonlight lit the lawn, and the outline of the gazebo shone in the darkness. "Yes, he wasn't happy about the attention I paid you. Talking to you at the gazebo was the greatest rebellion I ever committed against him. He never realized we spoke until later."

David chuckled again. "We didn't just chat, Bev. I can remember doing some parking out on Tyler Road."

Bev stood and waved his words away. She turned her back on him, facing out to the garden. She was either thinking hard or ignoring him.

He frowned at her, hating how she dismissed anything difficult or imperfect. But dammit, they had a grandkid here. They shouldn't spend the next eighteen years dancing around, ignoring each other.

Take tonight, for example. She required help, and he was the sole member of the family available. Still, she refused to speak.

"We don't need to talk about it." Her voice sounded solid, full of steel.

Anger flushed up his neck.

"Don't we?" he asked, pushing harder than he should.

Bev was not willing to engage in a serious conversation with David Kramer tonight. "I'll put Harper down. Then you can… continue your evening. Leave the crib…"

She'd been through enough surprises over the past few weeks. First, Father's death, though expected, hit her hard. Next, Cheryl showed up with a baby—and a Kramer baby at that. Afterward, her holidays had been interrupted and reorganized because she needed to do "family" events with the Kramers.

Having David thrown in her face every time she turned around felt unnerving. She needed to get away from him before she broke down completely. "I don't need you. Just go, David."

He looked at her.

The impact of her cold, sour words hit as she expected. His expression didn't change, but his gaze held a sad note.

That's what you get for dumping me, David. No sympathy.

"All right," he said, slowly standing with Harper in his arms. "I'll grab her car seat and go. Where is it?"

"Upstairs in the nursery."

David nodded and headed upstairs.

Bev followed in his wake, relieved he was leaving, but also wanting him to stay. Not because she was alone on New Year's Eve—she'd canceled the festivities when Father died. It didn't stop the rest of the family from running out to their own parties, though. Cheryl accepted an invitation from Ted, hence the babysitting. Will disappeared as usual, sending her a cryptic text about his whereabouts and the number for a car service he used as backup.

And Mother.

Mother had already left for a flight to the City to meet her cruise ship. Too soon to be gallivanting about, but Bev stopped trying years ago to make the woman behave.

Only Bev stayed home, like the dutiful daughter. Not partying, not celebrating—watching her grandchild... with her ex-fiancé.

Was he, though? She'd never answered him.

God, she didn't want to think about it, now or ever. And hadn't he just thrown it out there as if thirty-five years of heartbreak never happened? He should stop asking questions, stop making her uncomfortable, stop being better with Harper.

Upstairs, he paused at the door, and Bev realized he needed help. *Typical David. Not saying a word. Always expecting people to read his mind.*

She skirted around him and opened the door. She pulled the car seat from the corner and frowned.

"Is it safe for her to sleep in?" she asked, eyeing it with disdain.

"Asks the woman who almost put her in that." He pointed his chin at the pile of rubble that used to be a beautiful carriage.

She frowned, at both the destruction of the crib and David's nasty comment.

"Buckle her in, and you can go." She purposely threw extra ice into her words. *Enough nonsense.*

Moving delicately, he carefully lowered the sleeping child into the seat. *How had he been with his own boys?* The three never could've grown up so rowdy and loud if they'd been coddled by him. *David Kramer was no coddler, but look at him with the baby.*

With the utmost care, David buckled Harper into her seat. The baby sounded a few mewling noises, but did not wake.

"Now," he whispered, "she can stay there until the kids get her, or we can we rebuild the crib."

Bev glanced from him to the baby and back. "She looks uncomfortable, and I worry her head will be flat from sitting in it too much." *Why was she arguing? She wanted him to go, didn't she?* She threw her hands up.

He shook his head. "She's fine. If it makes you feel better, we can grab the mattress there and surround it with couch cushions. Toss a blanket on her, and she's good to go."

Bev's strength returned slightly. "No, no blankets. Cheryl said Harper rolls now. She'll tangle in it and strangle herself." She clutched at her throat. "We have to call the kids to come get her."

David sighed and gave her a weary look. "Or we could fix the crib, and she'd have a nice bed with fitted sheets."

Bev gazed at the mangled crib. Harper required a safe place to sleep. What choice did she have?

David watched Bev, measuring her response. From her body language, she absolutely didn't want the baby in the car seat, but she also wanted him gone. Guess tonight wasn't the night to end the feud.

He sighed.

"Give me an hour with the contraption." He waved, indicating the broken crib. "If I can't get it somewhat assembled, you can call the kids." He did not want to ruin Ted's night. The boy had been looking forward to a proper date with his girl for a long time.

David assumed Ted might even pop the question tonight. No doubt his son was ready for family life with Cheryl and Harper. Ted just needed to convince Cheryl to stay in Stonewater.

Fixing the crib and being nice to Bev was a small price to pay to help his kid find happiness. After the crap from the fire and Ryan's coming home, Ted had earned some happy. Hell, if Bev kept going on this way, David would just take Harper home.

Bev glanced at the baby in the seat one more time. With a resigned tone, she said, "Okay. How long will it take?"

David smiled, still plotting about talking to her. "Less than an hour, if you help me."

She gaped at him, her hand clutching her collar again. Damn, if he didn't want to buy her a string of pearls to complete the gesture.

"All right," she finally said. "I'll move her to my room so we don't wake her."

David considered carrying the heavy car seat for her, but Bev would never allow the likes of him near her room. He held the door open and waved her through.

Bev struggled, but managed to carry the girl out, returning in a few moments. "How loud will it be? Maybe Harper should go downstairs, and we could…"

He put a hand on her shoulder to stop the babbling. The woman over-planned everything. "No hammering, I promise. Harper will be fine."

Bev swallowed hard, but didn't move away. "Well, let's hurry up."

He smiled at her as he ran his hand down her arm to her fingertips and squeezed delicately. "Can ya hold the parts while I screw 'em together?"

Bev nodded blankly as he led her over to the crib pieces and squatted on the floor. He didn't need her. Well, maybe for those wagon wheels… Honestly, he could have it together in twenty minutes, but he lingered, like with the gazebo.

Once he studied the picture and examined the beast, he knew he could fix it easily with better screws. But he didn't tell Bev that.

She remained quiet and polite as he asked her to hold pieces together or hand him a tool. It was pure heaven to sit next to her and not fight.

After they worked for about five minutes, he asked, "So the elephant…"

He never could let anything lie. He poked at them until they bled. If he'd been smart, he would've fixed the crib, helped put the baby down, tipped his cap, and left. But nope, the feud ended now. The little one sleeping in the next room deserved it.

"Must we?" Bev asked, letting go of one of the metal railings.

David grabbed it before it hit the floor and clanged. "I think we gotta, Bev. This thing's gone on too long. Yell at me or berate me, but let's end it." He said the words while he focused on screwing the last piece of the metal frame together. They needed to add the bottom of the bed, followed by those arches and wheels. With the cage part together, Bev could put the mattress in it and have a spot for Harper tonight. If Beverly kicked him out for pressing her…

"David," she said, pulling away, but she didn't stand up. It seemed a good sign.

Images from Christmas Eve dinner flashed in his mind. A huge family, his family, sat at a dinner table. Multiple generations ate together with conversation and laughter. The day left him elated, seeing each of his boys with someone, and grandchildren, too. It was only a matter of time before all three boys married.

And Harper.

He'd never imagined anyone could fill his heart so completely. That little girl was their future, but he and Beverly needed to deal with their past.

When he'd repaired their gazebo, he'd been smitten and swooning over her like a love-sick teen. He'd proposed, expecting she'd never say yes, and her father would come after him for even talking to her. But her every glance made his heart flutter, so he'd asked.

She never said another word to him. His own father received a call, firing them from the job. The old man never reprimanded him, merely gave him a look, and told him to find other jobs to make up the money.

But he waited for Beverly, drove slowly past her house, frequented some of her haunts like the ice cream shop and the diner. Nothing. No Beverly, not for weeks.

Eventually, she remembered he existed, shooting him glaring looks if they passed on the street. Every time he tried to approach her, some rich boy or her father barred the way.

So he let it go.

She didn't want him, even after the flirting and fun. She probably had been slumming, and his heart paid the price.

Time for answers. He deserved at least that.

After sucking in a deep breath, he launched into another one of the stupid speeches he'd been making lately. He kept his head down, making it easier on both of them, and worked at putting the bottom on the baby cage.

"You never answered me, and, I guess, that was an answer. But it's always hurt me how you let your pa choose for you. I mean, it felt like ya did. He didn't like me and probably told you to stay away from me. I thought we had something…" He stopped, worried his voice held a tremble or another telling emotion. He didn't want to sound like a whiner. He merely wanted to understand why she left him and hated him for all this time.

"Fine," she said, her voice a little wavey. "Let's put the cards on the table."

Chapter Four

Bev took a deep breath and steadied herself. David concentrated on the crib, avoiding her gaze. Fine. He wanted to end the fight and ask the questions? Well, he'd have his answers. She would tell him the truth, and he'd have to deal with his cowardice.

"You asked me to marry you. You didn't ask my father." She spat out the words as she held up the first of the wagon wheels for him.

"Well, no…" His voice held confusion, but he never looked up from the crib.

Bev didn't wait. She plunged onward. "You were aware he didn't care for you, but you didn't stand up to him. I received a proposal, but you never asked him for my hand. I told him you loved me and asked me to marry you." She paused, hoping he would say something, but also wanting to continue.

"Hand me the screwdriver," was David's response. His head remained bowed over the crib. As usual, he said nothing.

She huffed but grabbed the requested tool.

He screwed in the first wheel and set up the next. "Hold this."

Anger bubbled in her stomach. *It's always this way with David.* He never spoke, never said anything. Never answered the big questions. Still holding the second wheel, she raged, "You did nothing. You didn't call or come by. I told him myself, and of course, he said no. He told me you weren't good enough, and he was right. You never came back for me when he refused. You never rescued me."

David glanced at her, sorrow in his gaze. He opened his mouth to speak, but Bev cut him off. She'd waited over thirty years to say it. He'd listen until she finished.

"You failed to be a standup guy, David Kramer. You don't ask a woman to marry you and then wander off. I was devastated, and you didn't care." She pulled away from him, not caring if the crib collapsed again.

She'd said it, finally told him how he had hurt her, abandoned her when she was so young. He had asked her to be his bride and never returned to the house. Not once. She'd waited for him, forgoing outings with friends in town, turning down requests for dates from more suitable men.

She sat for hours in the gazebo. Her hope waned with every passing hour, each day, that David didn't show to face her father. By the end of the summer, she became a crumbled shadow of herself. The first boy she loved had toyed with her heart and failed to rescue her from an oppressive father.

Finally, Father stepped in and asked her about her foul mood. He lectured her for days about the unacceptability of the Kramer family. By October, he convinced her a Kramer would never be good enough for a Winston. She accepted his opinion, but her broken heart never properly healed.

Now, the word "rescue" buzzed in her mind. David never rescued her back then, but he came to her aid tonight. She swallowed hard and stared at him.

David held a hand on the two-wheeled carriage and hung his head down. He sat that way for a moment, quiet as the grave, as always. He didn't move or twitch. After a second, he grabbed the third wheel and attached it to the crib.

Without a word.

The heat in Bev's blood boiled. *How dare he? How dare he sit there and not respond?* Her heart ached before the steel cage shut around it again.

Tossing him out looked like her best option. Tell him to leave and never come back. He wasn't interested in mending fences, only opening old wounds. How could she have ever loved such a callous person?

David continued assembling the crib, adding the fourth wheel at a much slower pace. Finally, he dropped the screwdriver, his chin on his chest.

"I'm so sorry, Beverly."

At first, he couldn't speak. Her words fell over him like a bucket of ice water and froze him to the core. She thought he'd abandoned her, that he hadn't been serious. His hands clenched into fists, remembering that summer. God, nothing was farther from the truth.

Back then, every instinct told him to run to her. But facing her father was futile unless Beverly stood with him. The man had fired him and sullied the Kramer name around town. David's own dad forbade him from seeing Beverly, even when David explained his feelings. He'd hoped Beverly felt the same for him, would stand up to her father, and come to him. David waited and waited, but she had been waiting for him, too.

Dammit.

He'd screwed it up, and the guilt rolled over him like an old rug. His jaw remained locked tight. He couldn't speak, didn't know how to express a genuine apology. It was too little, too late. He never planned to hurt her. He needed her to act, and she hadn't been able to. On some level, he understood, and fresh guilt hit his gut like a wrecking ball.

After grabbing the screwdriver, he fiddled with one of the wagon wheels. Busying his hands unlocked his tongue.

"I'm so sorry, Beverly," he managed to say. Shame rolled over him, forcing his gaze to remain on the floor. Would she understand why he did what he did? Probably not. If he'd known how badly she hurt, he would've fixed things long ago. For now, he'd try to explain, but no wonder she still hated him.

She stood, done with helping do the repair job.

With deference, he surrendered the high ground to her. He believed he'd done no wrong, but it didn't mean he didn't regret the consequences of his inaction. He should've fought harder.

Should is such a cop-out word.

"I…" He cleared his throat, took a breath, and started again. "I knew your pa hated me. He wouldn't have let me come calling. He'd never have said yes to my asking for your hand. I thought…" The words stuck in his windpipe again. "I thought you loved me enough to confront your father and stand up for me… Us. Tell him we were getting hitched whether he approved or not."

Slowly, he raised his head to meet her gaze.

Her blue eyes were twin sapphire lasers burning through him, and her mouth disappeared into a thin line.

He resisted the urge to demand why she never acted either, but arguing now solved nothing. He felt horrible, but she'd let him down just as hard.

"You didn't stand up for me, either." He whispered the words, trying not to sound accusatory or mean. She hadn't been the only one nursing a broken heart from the situation. *When your girl chooses her dad over you, maybe she didn't love you enough.*

Bev blinked at him. "You expected me to…" Her words began in a harsh tone, but it petered out. "My father…"

He looked at her and held out his hand. "I did wanna marry you, Bev. I loved ya. But I wanted you to be your own woman, too. Neither your dad or me shoulda been making choices for ya. You were always headstrong and confident. I thought you wouldn't want me to interfere with you and your pa. I counted on you confronting him. Beverly…" He grasped her hand with a gentle touch and guided her to sit with him. He squeezed her hand. "I'm sorry I hurt you. I never meant to."

She stared at him with wide, tear-filled eyes.

"I don't think you meant ta hurt me neither," he said.

She sucked in a breath, her free hand covering her mouth. A long blink sent those tears down her cheeks, and David felt a deep pull in his chest.

Her eyes still closed, she said, "No, I wanted you to stand up…"

"And I wanted you to do the same…"

They sat there on the floor, hand in hand, Bev quietly crying and David burning with guilt.

After a few minutes, he forced himself to move. Sitting on the floor and wallowing didn't do either of them any good. He stood and pulled her up with him. "I think it's stable enough for Harper. Wanna put her in?"

Bev nodded meekly. He hated the gesture instantly. The woman was usually all fire and brimstone. He hated a cowed Bev.

"Are you sure it will hold? We didn't put all the parts on." She waved at the metal arches that were supposed to crisscross over the crib, creating the top of the carriage.

David scrubbed his chin. "They seem more decoration." He pushed the crib against the wall and pressed down on the bottom. Stable. He grabbed the sides and rocked it a bit, and the thing held.

"One sleepy baby won't crash it tonight." He smiled at her, hoping she'd lighten a little.

Bev blinked at him.

His shoulders fell. "I'll throw the mattress in, and you go get her. We'll see what happens."

Bev left the room as if walking in a fog.

David watched her go, praying his words meant something to her. He dared not hope for forgiveness, but an understanding of their past might go a long way to ease the tension between them. Hell, he'd pardoned her years ago. And after tonight, any lingering animosity disappeared. They might actually be friends now, for more than Harper's sake.

He set the mattress in the crib. A rummage through the dresser and closet turned up a fitted sheet with tiny stars dancing over it. He tucked it in and replaced the bumper cushions around the sides.

Bev came in as he tied the last cushion onto the metal grid. She set the carrier down. Harper slept on, oblivious to the movement or the change in the atmosphere in the nursery.

Bev crossed her arms and stepped back. "Well, it looks safe." Her voice was a mere wisp.

David caught her gaze and smiled reassuringly. "We'll know soon enough." Carefully, he unbuckled the sleeping baby and lifted her from the car seat.

Harper groaned and smacked her lips.

David moved like a turtle, slowly, carefully, with tiny steps until he stood over the crib. He glanced at Bev, who waved her crossed fingers. He grinned and lowered the baby into the crib.

They both waited, breath held, bodies tense and ready to grab the child from the bed if it collapsed again.

Harper, on her back, stretched her arms over her head and sighed. The cutest sound he ever heard.

A hand pressed on his shoulder, and he glanced over to witness Bev smiling down on their grand babe. A tremendous weight fell off his shoulders and shattered around them.

Bev breathed a sigh of relief. Miracle of miracles, David managed to put Harper down without a blip from the child. He really was a baby whisperer. She stood over his shoulder, watching the little girl. She glanced at him and realized she'd put a hand on his shoulder. A warm sensation cascaded up her arm. She forced herself to repress a wide smile.

She slipped her hand down his arm and gave a little tug. If they hoped to keep the baby asleep, they needed to duck out quickly and quietly.

He understood and followed her out of the room.

Once outside, she left the door open a crack and faced David.

"I'll get those tools another day," he said.

She'd forgotten his toolbox. With her hand on her forehead, she said, "I'm sorry. If you want to go back…"

He shook his head. "No way. If I clanked one tool, she'd be awake and yellin'. It can wait."

They headed downstairs, and Bev moved to retrieve his coat. Words eluded her. *What do you say after that?* She had gotten answers after so many years, but processing was another matter.

He'd never meant to hurt her, only wanted good things for her. In the end, his pain equaled hers. The fact that he said he was sorry, instead of defending himself and fighting as she'd expected… it threw her. Most men did not open with an apology. Most men were not David Kramer.

Her hand trembled as she handed him the coat. The burning fire of hatred inside her cooled, smothered by his apology. She didn't want him to go. She considered asking him to stay for coffee, to talk, to mend more fences. Honestly, she hadn't felt this calm in years. But sitting with him alone in her parlor sounded like too much, too soon.

He accepted the coat with quiet thanks. His gaze met hers. "I could come by tomorrow and finish the crib. At least, get the tools." He flashed her a half-smile as if feeling out the new amiability between them.

"Sounds good, David. Perhaps if you come at noon, we'll have lunch with Harper. You're the expert at feeding her, after all." Another chain broke from around her heart as he looked at her. His eyes sparkled, and his smile beamed.

"I'll be here. Thank you, Beverly."

They stared into each other's eyes for a moment before Bev glanced away. She needed to process everything. After each of their confessions, a truce stood within their grasps. She could forgive him. He'd tried to be a good man, and she had misunderstood his actions. Had she come down off her high horse just once, they've buried the hatchet years ago. That was on both of them, like their break-up, like their reconciliation. Heat rose in her cheeks as her brain digested the word. What might happen now that she understood the truth?

"Thank you, David."

She led him to the door and opened it.

He paused and said, "Happy New Year, Bev," and brushed his lips across her cheek.

Heat flushed down her neck, and she considered spending the rest of the evening with him.

Another time...

He walked away without another word. She stood in the doorway, her hand on her cheek, a new future ahead of them.

The End

Love the this story?

Go back to the beginning with *Christmas Sparks*!

Christmas Sparks

Chapter One

Shin-deep in the December snow, Ryan Kramer wiped an ash-covered hand across his forehead. *Goddamn holiday fires.* Black smoke still poured out of the white colonial, despite the best efforts of the Stonewater volunteer fire brigade. The fire danced with a will of its own, sending thick gray smoke skyward. If the blaze spread to the second floor, he and his fellow firefighters were in for a long night.

Someone tugged on his jacket.

He glanced down at a soot-smeared boy. The child pointed to the house. His bottom lip trembled as a tear rolled down his cheek.

"My mommy's inside." His voice sounded raspy from the heated air. The boy dropped his hand slowly as ash and snow fell on his shoulders. His chattering teeth spoke more of shock than cold.

"You sure, bud?" Ryan knelt to meet the child's gaze. The little guy looked only about five or six. He and the other firefighters had cleared the house. Two kids, one woman. If she went back in… Ryan's pulse quickened as he prepared to don the ventilator again.

The boy stared at his home, tears in his eyes. "Yeah, I'm sure." The words were barely out of his mouth before a shriek pierced the air.

"Mikey! There you are." A young teen rushed over and crushed the kid in her arms. "Jesus, shrimp. I thought you…" Her gaze met Ryan's, and she switched to Indifferent Mode. "Whatever. You're safe. Stay here." Her words sounded aloof, but she didn't let go of the child.

Ryan touched Mikey's arm to get the boy's attention back. "Your mother, where is she?" The girl glanced around. Mikey pointed to the house again.

"Mikey." The teen knelt in the snow. "Mom went back inside?" He nodded, and she paled. The sound of breaking glass filled the air as a window blew out. Both kids flinched, huddling closer, tears on their cheeks.

Time to act. "Upstairs or down, Mikey?"

"Up?" he asked, his voice muffled as he buried his head in his sister's shoulder. Ryan glanced at the girl, who shrugged.

"Stay here," he ordered, waving an EMT over to the children. Dashing toward the house, he called to Chief Burges. "Woman, second floor." He tugged the self-contained breathing apparatus, or SCBA mask, into position over his mouth and slapped his helmet back on. After a deep breath, he burst through the smoky doorway.

Inside, thick gray clouds billowed from the living room. Two volunteers worked to contain the blaze in the room. He caught their attention, pointed at himself then the stairs. The guys paused for a thumbs-up.

A woman upstairs? How had she snuck past everyone? It didn't matter. He needed to find her, get her out.

Now.

Rushing up the wooden steps, Ryan almost removed the SCBA to call out. Taking it off inside a burning building was a violation and a stupid move. Somehow, he'd find her. His pulse quickened as he climbed to the top of the stairwell, instinct pushing him faster. Rooms stood to the left and right of the stairs.

He'd fought many fires in Meadow Wood Estates. The master bedroom always sat on the right side of the house. His gut told him to head there. Smoke gathered around his head. The door to the master stood ajar, and he nudged it open.

The murky room appeared empty at first glance. Stepping through the doorway, he peered through the haze, looking for any movement. A cough caught his attention. He swung around. In the dim light, he spotted a woman scrabbling through files on an old oak desk.

"Hey," he called, the SCBA muffling his words. "The house is on fire!"

She jumped, spinning around, her arms full of papers. "What?" she asked, blinking. Soot marred her pale skin, and ash and water spattered her clothes. Dust peppered her dark hair.

"You gotta leave," he yelled through the SCBA.

Tilting her head coyly, she said, "One second, please," The sweet, calm authority of her words stymied Ryan and he stopped in his tracks. Her reaction was the absolute opposite of what he expected. Then she flashed him a smile.

The simple beauty of it rocked him on his heels. All thoughts disappeared from his mind. He could only stare at that smile, that face, thunderstruck.

He almost answered, "Oh, okay," to her melodious and endearing tone. The crackling of the fire downstairs snapped him back to reality. Quickly, he crossed to the desk where she hunkered, sorting paperwork.

"I'll be two shakes." She continued to move and stack documents, adding more to the pile in her arms.

"Yeah, no." He wrapped his arms around her waist, lifted, and spun her around. *They don't call it a fireman's carry for nothing.*

The woman shrieked. Hefting her on his shoulder, he hurried out the door and to the hallway. She kicked, screamed, and cursed, her sweet, quiet tone replaced by something demonic. Twice while on the stairs, she almost hurled them to the bottom with her squirming.

All the fuss only made him admire her more.

"Lady, read me the riot act later." He adjusted her position, purposely bouncing her slightly. Papers floated around them.

"No!" Her voice cut through the air like a siren. "I need those. Stop."

Ryan continued down the stairs.

"Stop now." She commanded, and once again he almost obeyed. She kicked out, inches short of crushing his nuts. The glancing blow against his coat woke him from his trance.

"No," he said, adding authority in his tone. "Paper's replaceable. You aren't."

She huffed but quieted to a disgruntled mutter. Who was this chick? Sweet one minute, then swearing like a sailor, next ordering him around like a sergeant.

A call of alarm sounded from the living room where the guys still battled the blaze. A command, mixed with panic in their voices, sounded like "Gas line!" Ryan didn't wait to find out the rest. Gripping the woman tighter, he hurried out the front door and onto the lawn.

The surrounding air sizzled. Then a huge boom filled their ears. A wall of pressure smashed into them. His feet left the ground, and the universe clicked into slow motion. Acting on instinct, he twisted, curling the woman into his chest. She squeaked as they tumbled headlong into the snow.

His back crashed against the piled snow on the lawn. Her weight smashed against his torso, forcing the breath from his lungs. He closed his eyes for a beat, screaming a mental *"Oww."* When she groaned in his arms, his training kicked in.

Rolling over quickly, but gently, he placed the woman on the snow. He knocked off his helmet and shoved the SCBA to the side, scanning her up and down for injuries.

Haloed by the gleaming snow, the thirty-something woman with pale skin stared up at him. Her pretty face shone pink with exertion. Her brown eyes sparkled with unspoken fury, or maybe fear, as she gasped for breath. Papers scattered around her like rose petals on a bed.

Something deep inside him opened up and his heart called out. He swallowed hard, trying to resist the call of insta-love.

Leaning over her, restraining the rush of lust, he asked, "Are you all right, miss?" Her gaze remained blank, her lips twitching. He should've been concerned about a head injury, but his testosterone-soaked brain said, "gorgeous." It didn't help they were pressed together in the snow. "Miss?"

Slowly, her liquid brown eyes fixed on his, the faraway stare fading. With seemingly great effort, she raised a hand to his cheek, her face tilting slightly.

The instinct to kiss her surged in his chest and other areas, but he held back. Her lips opened, and Ryan believed he'd found the woman of his dreams. Rescuing her from a fire, saving her life…

She placed her whole hand over his face and shoved him away—rather unexpected, considering the romantic tension in the air. *Thank God, she didn't dig her nails in.*

Ryan's mouth hung open, words failing.

She, on the other hand, had no problem speaking her mind. "What the hell do you think you're doing?" She heaved him off her and stood up.

"The fire, miss. I… I was rescuing you."

She snorted, her hands on her hips. "I was fine. You didn't need to do a dramatic rescue. This isn't some romance novel." She marched toward the house, but Ryan caught her arm.

His desire dissolved into anger. This woman took the cake for belligerent rescues. "Did you not hear the explosion?"

Grabbing his arm, she hauled him to his feet. Ryan blinked at her in surprise.

"Are my kids okay?" Ah, Mama Bear Syndrome. He pointed to two small figures dashing toward them.

"Yep." It was the only syllable he managed before she turned on him again.

"I know you. You're one of those Kramers, aren't you? Figures."

Ryan stepped back. Over the years, his father and his contracting company hadn't always done its best for their customers. Ryan had left Stonewater to escape his family's tainted shadow. But now, it dropped over him again. It didn't matter he'd pulled her from a fire.

"Mommy!" Mikey slammed into the woman, wrapping his arms tight around her thighs. She wavered for a second from the impact. Kneeling, she engulfed the boy in her arms, kissing his forehead, checking him for injuries, whispering words of reassurance. But the reunion didn't squelch her anger at Ryan.

"Your family is responsible for this mess." She waved at the house. "It's December. My house blew up with everything inside. Our Christmas things are gone. Where will we stay?" She threw her chin up, glaring, but tears glistened in her eyes.

Dammit. She was out on the street with two kids—at Christmas. "Your husband?" he asked tentatively.

She blew a raspberry. An actual raspberry. "Now, what am I going to do?"

"Geez, Ma," the daughter said. "Give the guy a break. He did carry you out, caveman-style. Kinda sexy." She flashed her phone. "I got it on vid. Man, my friends are gonna freak." She turned her back on the adults, clicking her phone at the house, the firemen, and snapping several selfies.

"Jill, please." Her mother ran her fingers through her daughter's hair. "Oh, God, the paperwork." She sank to her knees and gathered up some of the scattered sheets. "If it's not here, if I could lose…" A tiny sob halted her words.

Ryan's heartstrings twanged again. He glanced at the woman, her two kids, and the burning house highlighting the snowy ground. Regret filled his gut. Having saved her life, he needed to go save her house. Before heading into the smoke, he asked, "Why did you go back, miss? For papers?"

She glared up at him, those brown eyes molten. Her nose wrinkled, but before she could speak, her son piped up. "You got my picture? Thanks, Mommy."

Mikey scooped up a crayon family portrait, complete with a Christmas tree.

She pushed a strand of hair away from the kid's eyes. "Of course, I did, sweetie."

Ryan gulped. A woman who'd risk her life for her kid's drawing…There was something in that—strong and a bit insane. His heart fell. It didn't matter. She'd hired his dad to work on the house. She'd never give Ryan the time of day ever again.

"I'll send the EMTs over to look at you," he said cordially, donning his helmet.

"I'm fine. Thank you," she spat, wrapping her kids in her arms.

To be continued…

Download or purchase Christmas Sparks at your favorite bookseller

Also by Ginny Frost

The Oakwood Tavern Series

The Bar Scene, Oakwood Tavern 1

Terese Brock manages the Oakwood Tavern with style and grace. Unfortunately, she's trying to avoid her employer's IRS disaster and her own debts. She needs a new job—fast. Terese hopes to land an executive position at the new conference center, the perfect solution to all her money woes.

For months, Drew Drake has admired Terese from afar, but she doesn't know he exists. He's thrilled when his humor and persistence catch her eye. And when she takes him home, he discovers she's everything he expected, and so much more.

Drew fails to mention he's the heir to one of the most successful businesses in town, the force behind the new conference center. Rather than clue her in, he decides to let her get to know the real him. When she walks into her interview, ready to kick ass and take names, her universe shatters.

Behind the desk sits her boy-toy, Drew.

Swindled, Oakwood Tavern 2

For years, Marley Volkov's survival depended on conning people out of their life savings. One look into Alan Reid's pained eyes, with his soiled reputation and heap of financial problems, awakens a new empathy inside her. She renounces grifting forever and not just because every inch of her burns to be with him. But his association with her and her checkered past will drag him further into the gutter. To save herself, to save him, she must walk away. Walk away from the unbridled desire he inspires, from the passion and sympathy that feel like home.

Alan Reid is buried to the neck in money issues. The understanding and compassion he finds in Marley is the exact thing he needs at the completely wrong time. Everything about her makes his blood run hot. She's smart, irresistible, and a criminal. Why is the only person who's ever shown him sympathy have to be a con artist? He can't be with her, but he's compelled to save her from herself.

Stranded, Oakwood Tavern 3

Where the hell is Conrad?

While his business partners back at The Oakwood Tavern think he's on the run for tax evasion, for Conrad Bennett, it's a whole other story. One that includes being stranded on an island in the South Pacific with no cell phone, no money, and no passport.

Good thing he just slept with the only woman on the island with a plane.

Vivian Costa has her own problems. She's on this remote island for a much needed, much overdue, self-imposed exile. But now her one-night stand wants not only a ride off the island, but to find out who has set him up. So much for laying low and hiding out. Vivian knows she should walk away, but there's something about Conrad that won't let her.

It's time to figure out how to rescue each other.

When Hearts Collide, Oakwood Tavern 4

Planning and organizing the wedding this weekend left Stacey Montgomery little time for fun. She's woefully behind on her Bucket List from the bridal shower. Right now, on the plane to Massachusetts, it's her last chance to cross off number three. Luckily, there's a hottie sitting next to her, and he looks promising. And if her plan succeeds, she might invite him for all the other winter activities on the list.

After working through a criminal IRS audit at his job in Iverton, Eric Holmes could use some rest and relaxation. Usually, bad luck plows him flat like a steamroller, but this time his friend Pete caught the bad juju. With his bestie in a cast from a skiing accident, Eric gladly took Pete's place to tend bar at a destination wedding on the Atlantic coast. Then, he sat next to the most beautiful woman —blonde, curvy, and…

She just asked him to join the mile-high club

Gulp.

But how can he say no?

Stonewater Stories

The Carriage House, Stonewater Stories Book 0.5

Homeless, jobless, and newly single, Cheryl Winston-Bristol finds herself back at her oppressive childhood home. Even at the Carriage House of their estate, she can't escape her overbearing mother and tyrant of a grandfather from making her life miserable. That is until she discovers her high school crush, Ted Kramer, repairing the steps. The dozen years of handyman repairs have molded him into quite a hunk.

Ted working around her house every day? Yes, thank you.

Desperate for the work, Ted Kramer of Kramer and Sons agreed to take the job at the Winston-Bristol's Carriage House. Ted is both excited and terrified since most of their family hates his. Then he discovers Cheryl is home and living in the Carriage House. Working in the same place with the beautiful, classy Cheryl terrifies and excites him. He can handle seeing the charming Cheryl all summer, can't he?

In this prequel to the Stonewater Stories, learn how Ted and Cheryl found each other. To hear their happily ever after, read all of the Stonewater Stories.

Christmas Sparks, Stonewater Stories Book 1

Kindergarten teacher, Margaret Porter, is looking forward to the best Christmas holiday in years. Without her irresponsible ex-husband causing chaos, she and her two children can finally have a fun, peaceful celebration. Everything looks picture perfect until her living room catches fire.

Volunteer firefighter, Ryan Kramer, never knew what hit him when he rescues a reluctant and quick-tempered Margaret from her burning home. But it's more than sympathy for her situation that gets under his skin. Her sassy, no-nonsense attitude bowls him over.

Margaret finds her family rescued by Ryan again and again. Something about him speaks to her soul, and she discovers it hard to resist him. Unlike her careless and manipulative ex-husband, Ryan's nothing but wonderful throughout the entire ordeal.

As Ryan investigates the damage to Margaret's home, he discovers his family's business, Kramer and Sons, worked on the fire-ravaged room. Did shoddy work by his family put a single mom and her two kids out in the cold at Christmas? Can Margaret see beyond his last name and fall for him too?

Christmas Affair, Stonewater Stories Book 2

Josephine Lockwood spent her entire life in a sickbed being coddled by her anxious mother. Finally, after receiving the correct diagnosis for her illness, she's standing on the edge of a new adventure. She's finished her audition program for an online gaming platform and is poised to move out of her family home. But she must attend her mother's annual Christmas party.

Brett Kramer, a hard-working handyman, is finishing up renovations at the Excelsior Hotel in Iverton when Jo drops into his life. She's cute, friendly, and totally intriguing. Too bad he's at work. The family contracting business is suffering thanks to a bogus complaint, and he doesn't want any whiff of impropriety to taint the current contract.

But when Jo flees from her mother's party, Brett steps in to help her escape, disregarding his business's reputation.

Their departure only complicates the situation. A snowstorm, sibling rivalry, and an overprotective mother forces them together and tears them apart. Jo and Brett must find a balance to make their relationship more than a Christmas Affair.

Christmas Baby, Stonewater Stories Book 3

He'd heard the rumors she was back in town. He had to see for himself.

As Ted Kramer steeled himself to knock on the hotel room door, the last thing he was prepared to see was the woman who shattered him holding a baby. Cheryl Winston-Bristol had been the love of his life. And when she abruptly left town last year after their secret summer romance, it destroyed him. He couldn't eat. Couldn't sleep. Couldn't work. Yet here she is, baby and all. His baby. Merry Christmas to him.

When Cheryl realized she was pregnant, she knew her controlling and manipulative grandfather would never accept a Kramer child into his family. The feud between the Kramers and Winston-Bristols had dragged on for forty years and as long as that cantankerous man was alive, it would continue raging. Except now he's dead, and Cheryl has taken the opportunity to return to Stonewater for the services. She knows she needs to tell her mother-- and Ted-- about the baby, but she never wanted him to find out about his daughter like this, though.

Maybe, just maybe, baby Harper will be the Christmas gift these families need to move on and find love again.

The Mortar & Pestle Series
Artist: A Second Chance Romance

Lexi Pintari is stuck in a dead-end cubicle job that is slowly killing her. She tucked away her passion for art when the love of her life ghosted her after college. Witnessing her lack of motivation, Lexi's best friend drags her to an art retreat for much-needed reflection and inspiration. Though knowing her ex-boyfriend is an artist-in-residence there, Lexi agrees to go. Unfortunately, her metal-goth style and enthusiasm for graphic comics clash with the pastel-scarf-wearing, tea-sipping participants, making her ex the least of her problems.

Cole MacDougall is blocked. His rise to the top of the modern art scene is crushed by a missing muse. He is desperate to paint again, but the canvas remains blank. Due to the shortage of patronage revenue, he is forced to put up with the groupie-students. Until he sees a woman standing out like a sore thumb in ripped jeans and a leather jacket. Lexi. Hope blooms that he can renew his passion through her.

About the Author

Ginny Frost is an indie author with three great series. She writes contemporary romance with a sexy, funny kick. In her downtime, she plays clerk at the local library—the perfect job to feed her reading addiction.

She lives in upstate NY with her very own kindhearted ogre, their two brilliant and creative children, and an evil cat named Flash.

Find Ginny Frost online

www.ginnyfrost.com

.